Peter Pan

My First Classics

A Little Princess

by Frances Hodgson Burnett,

adapted by Laura F. Marsh

The Secret Garden

by Frances Hodgson Burnett,

adapted by Laura F. Marsh

Anne of Green Gables

by L. M. Montgomery,

adapted by Laura F. Marsh

Black Beauty

by Anna Sewell,

adapted by Laura F. Marsh

My First Classics

Peter Pan

By J. M. Barrie

Adapted by Laura F. Marsh

HarperFestival®
A Division of HarperCollins*Publishers*

My First Classics: Peter Pan

Printed in the United States.

www.harperchildrens.com
Library of Congress catalog card number: 2005931028
ISBN-10: 0-06-079149-7 — ISBN-13: 978-0-06-079149-0
Typography by Tom Starace
1 2 3 4 5 6 7 8 9 10
❖
First HarperFestival edition, 2006

Contents

Peter Pan

1

Peter Breaks Through

Except for one child named Peter Pan, all children grow up. Children understand that everyone grows up eventually, and so did Wendy.

Wendy lived in London with her parents, Mr. and Mrs. Darling, and her two brothers, John and Michael. After Wendy was born, Mr. and Mrs. Darling were worried about being able to feed another mouth. But then John arrived, and then Michael. And the family managed to get along quite well.

Mrs. Darling loved to have everything just so. And Mr. Darling wanted to be exactly like their neighbors, so they had a nurse for their children like everyone else in the neighborhood.

Since they did not have extra money to spend, their nurse was a Newfoundland dog called Nana. She proved to be a treasure of a nurse. She was quite thorough at bath time and got up in the middle of the night whenever one of the children made the slightest cry. Of course, her kennel was in the nursery so she could be close to the children.

It was a wonder to watch Nana walk the children to school. She would walk slowly by their sides if they were well behaved. But she would nudge them back into line if they strayed. When there was a chance of rain, she carried an umbrella in her mouth. Nana was always well prepared.

No children's nurse, dog or human, could have done a better job, and Mr. Darling knew it. Yet sometimes he was concerned that the neighbors were talking about his family behind their backs.

However, there was not a happier family than the Darlings. They had such fun dancing in the nursery together. Nana would dance around the room in her maid's cap, and Mrs. Darling would twirl and pirouette wildly. Until Peter Pan arrived, all was well.

Mrs. Darling had first heard of Peter Pan in her childhood. There were odd stories about Peter, and she had heard that he lived with fairies. Mrs. Darling had believed in Peter when she was young, but now that she was married and grown-up, she doubted there had been any such person.

One day when Wendy and Mrs. Darling were talking, the subject of Peter Pan came up.

"Well," Mrs. Darling said, "he would be grown-up now."

"Oh, no, he isn't," said Wendy. "He is just my size."

Mrs. Darling was alarmed and spoke to Mr. Darling about it.

"Peter Pan is just some nonsense Nana has put in their heads. It will blow over soon," Mr. Darling told his wife.

But it did not blow over. A little while later, the troublesome Peter Pan gave Mrs. Darling quite a shock.

One morning, Mrs. Darling made a discovery: some leaves were found on the nursery floor, and they had not been there when the children had gone to bed the night before. Mrs. Darling was puzzling over the leaves when Wendy entered the room.

"I guess it is that Peter Pan again!" Wendy said with a smile.

"What do you mean, dear?" Mrs. Darling asked.

Her daughter explained casually that she thought Peter sometimes came to the nursery at night, sat on the foot of her bed, and played his pipes. Unfortunately, Wendy said, she never woke up, so she didn't know how she knew this. She just did.

"Nonsense! No one can get into the house without knocking," Mrs. Darling said quite nervously.

"I think he comes in the window," said Wendy calmly.

"But it's three floors up," Mrs. Darling declared.

"Weren't the leaves in front of the window?" Wendy asked.

It was true. They had been found right there. Mrs. Darling did not know what to think. It all seemed so natural to Wendy.

"My child," said Mrs. Darling, "why didn't you tell me this before?"

"I forgot," Wendy said lightly. She hurried downstairs to breakfast.

Mrs. Darling looked carefully at the leaves again. She was sure they did not come from any tree in England. She so wished her daughter had been dreaming. But the very next night proved that Wendy had not been dreaming. For that was when the extraordinary adventures of the Darling children began.

On that night, all the children were safely in bed. It was Nana's evening off of work, so Mrs. Darling had given the children a bath and put them to bed. She sang to them until one by one they drifted off to sleep.

As she sat down by the fire to sew, Mrs. Darling felt safe and cozy looking at her children. The nursery was dimly lit by three night-lights. As Mrs. Darling sewed, her head drooped, and she fell asleep.

While she slept, Mrs. Darling had a dream. She dreamed that Neverland, the land of children's dreams, had come too close and a strange boy had broken through from it. As she was dreaming, the nursery window blew open and a boy dropped onto the floor.

With the boy was a strange light no bigger than a fist. The light darted about the room like a living thing. It was the light that awakened Mrs. Darling.

When she saw the boy, Mrs. Darling jumped with a cry. Somehow she knew it was Peter Pan. He was dressed in leaves, and she could see that he had all his baby teeth.

When Peter saw that there was a grown-up in the room, he gnashed his pearly teeth at Mrs. Darling.

2

The Shadow

Mrs. Darling screamed. As if in answer, the door opened and Nana came rushing in. She growled and sprang at the boy, who leaped quickly out the window. Again Mrs. Darling screamed, this time because she thought he had fallen three stories to the street below.

She ran down to the street to look for his little body, but it was not there. As she looked up, she could see nothing in the night sky, except what she thought was a shooting star.

Mrs. Darling returned to the nursery and found Nana had something in her mouth. It was the boy's shadow. As the boy had leaped out the window, Nana had closed it too quickly. Down had come the window and it snapped off the boy's shadow.

As you can imagine, Mrs. Darling looked at the shadow carefully, but it was the ordinary kind. She did not know what to do with it. She thought of showing it to Mr. Darling, but she knew what he would say: "It's all because we have a dog for a nurse."

So Mrs. Darling decided to roll the shadow up and put it away in a drawer. Eventually she would find a way to tell her husband about it. This happened one week later on that never-to-be-forgotten Friday.

"I ought to have been more careful," Mrs. Darling would say afterward to her husband. And he would hold one of her hands and Nana would hold the other.

"No, no, no," Mr. Darling would tell her. "It was my fault."

They sat like that in the empty nursery every night after that terrible Friday. They remembered each small detail of what had happened that evening.

"If only I had not accepted the dinner invitation at our neighbors at Number Twenty-Seven," Mrs. Darling said.

"If only I had not poured my medicine into Nana's bowl," said Mr. Darling.

Then one or both of them would start to cry. Even Nana would cry real tears, and Mr. Darling would hold a handkerchief up to her eyes.

That terrible night had begun just like any other night. Nana had given the children a bath. Mrs. Darling had come into the room wearing her white evening gown for the dinner party. She had dressed early because Wendy so loved to see her in fancy clothes. Once Mr. Darling was dressed, he danced around the room with young Michael on his back. They had a delightful time.

That night, Mrs. Darling had shown her husband the boy's shadow. At first Mr. Darling didn't want to believe the story, but then he became quite thoughtful when she showed him the shadow.

"It is no one I know," Mr. Darling had said, "but he does look like a scoundrel."

They were still discussing the shadow when Nana came in with Michael's medicine. Michael did everything he could to avoid the spoon of medicine in Nana's mouth. This annoyed Mr. Darling.

"I won't take it!" cried Michael naughtily.

"Michael, when I was your age, I took medicine without a sound," said Mr. Darling. "I thanked my parents for giving it to me so I would get well. The medicine that I take now is much nastier than yours. I would show you how well I take it if I had not lost the bottle."

The truth was that Mr. Darling had not lost the bottle. He had really hidden it in his wardrobe.

"I know where it is," said Wendy helpfully. "I'll bring it to you." And so she did. When Wendy returned, Mr. Darling promised to take his medicine at the same time as Michael. But he did not. Actually he would try just about anything to avoid taking his medicine as well. The children were not happy with him.

"Look here," said the desperate Mr. Darling. "I have just thought of a splendid joke. I will pour my medicine in Nana's bowl, and she will drink it since it looks like milk."

The children looked at him in a scolding way. They did not think this was a good idea. But Mr. Darling poured the nasty liquid into Nana's bowl anyway.

"Oh, George!" cried Mrs. Darling.

"It was only a joke," Mr. Darling said in his defense. "I'm trying so hard to be funny in this house, but no one appreciates it."

"George, not so loud," said Mrs. Darling. "There's nothing to get upset about."

That just made Mr. Darling even angrier. He felt that the dog got more respect than he did. "The proper place for that dog is in the yard," he yelled. "I'm going to tie you up right now, Nana."

"George," Mrs. Darling whispered, "remember what I told you about that boy Peter Pan." She thought Nana should be near the children in case Peter returned.

But Mr. Darling would not listen. He was determined to show who was master in the house—and it wasn't the dog. He took Nana from the nursery and headed outside to tie her up. Even as he did it, he was ashamed of himself.

In the meantime, Mrs. Darling put the children to bed and lit their night-lights. They could hear Nana barking.

"That is not Nana's unhappy bark," Wendy said. "That is her bark when she smells danger."

"Danger! Are you sure, Wendy?" cried Mrs. Darling.

"Yes," she replied.

Mrs. Darling shivered and went to the window. It was securely locked. She looked out, and the night was peppered with stars. They were crowding around the house, curious to see what was to take place there. But Mrs. Darling did not notice this.

She did notice a fear that clutched her heart, though. "Oh, I wish that I wasn't going to the party tonight!" she said aloud.

Even Michael sensed that she was fearful. "Can anything harm us, Mother, after the lights are out?" he asked.

"Nothing, dear," replied Mrs. Darling. She went from bed to bed, singing to her children softly.

Little Michael threw his arms around her. "I'm glad of you!" he said. They were the last words she heard from him for a long time.

The house at Number 27 was only a few yards away. All the stars were watching Mr. and Mrs. Darling as they walked down the street. Once the Darlings entered the door of their neighbors', the smallest of all the stars cried out, "Now, Peter!"

3

Wendy and Peter

For a moment after Mr. and Mrs. Darling left the house, the night-lights by the children's beds continued to burn brightly. But quickly all three lights went out.

There was another light in the room now—much brighter than the night-lights had been. It was going in and out of all the drawers in the nursery, looking for Peter's shadow. And when it came to rest for a moment, you could see it was a fairy no longer than your hand. Her name was Tinker Bell, and she was wearing a beautiful gown.

A moment after the fairy entered the room, the window blew open and Peter dropped onto the floor of the nursery.

"Tinker Bell," Peter called softly. "Do you know where they put my shadow?"

The loveliest tinkle of golden bells answered him. This sound was the fairy language.

Tink told Peter that the shadow was in the big chest of drawers. So he ran and found it. But in his excitement, he forgot Tink and shut her in a drawer. Peter did not notice his mistake.

When his shadow did not stick right back on, Peter was surprised. He tried to stick his shadow back on with soap from the bathroom, but that didn't work. He was so upset that he sat on the floor and cried.

His sobs woke Wendy, and she sat up in bed. She was not alarmed to see a stranger crying on the nursery floor. Instead she was pleasantly interested.

"Boy," she said kindly, "why are you crying?"

Peter could be very polite, for he had learned good manners at fairy ceremonies. He rose and bowed to Wendy beautifully. She was very pleased and bowed to him from the bed.

"What's your name?" he asked.

"Wendy Moira Angela Darling," she replied. "What is your name?"

"Peter Pan," he responded.

Then Wendy asked where he lived.

"Second to the right," said Peter, "and then straight on till morning."

"What a funny address," exclaimed Wendy. "Is that what they put on your letters?"

"I don't get any letters," said Peter.

"But your mother gets letters?" Wendy asked.

"I don't have a mother," he answered. He did not think mothers were necessary anyway. Wendy, however, thought this was very sad indeed.

"Oh, Peter, no wonder you were crying," she said. Wendy got out of bed and ran to him.

"I wasn't crying about mothers," said Peter in his defense. "I was crying because I can't get my shadow back on."

Then Wendy saw the shadow on the floor and she felt terribly sorry for him. "How awful!" she cried, but she could not help smiling when she saw that he had been trying to stick it back on with soap.

Fortunately Wendy knew exactly what to do. "It must be sewn on," she said knowingly. So she sewed on the shadow and Peter was delighted. He jumped about with glee. He had already forgotten that it was Wendy who had fixed his problem.

"How clever I am!" he crowed.

Wendy was shocked. "I was the one who fixed your shadow!"

"You helped a little," replied Peter carelessly as he continued to dance around the room.

"A little!" Wendy exclaimed. She hopped into bed angrily and pulled the blankets over her head.

Peter sat on the end of the bed and tapped her gently on the foot. "Wendy," he said, "don't be angry. I can't help crowing when I'm pleased with myself."

Wendy would not look up, but she was listening underneath the blankets. "Wendy, one girl is more use than twenty boys," said Peter.

Wendy could not help peeking out of the covers. "Do you really think so?" she asked.

"Yes, I do," he answered.

"That's very sweet," she said. Wendy sat with him on the side of the bed. She said she would give Peter a kiss if he liked, but Peter did not know what she meant. He held out his hand.

"Surely you know what a kiss is," Wendy said, shocked.

"I will know when you give it to me," Peter replied.

So as not to hurt his feelings, Wendy put a thimble in his outstretched hand.

"Now," he said, "shall I give you a kiss?"

"If you please," she replied primly. Peter dropped an acorn button in her hand. Wendy said she would wear the kiss on the chain around her neck. It was lucky that she did, for that acorn would save her life some time later.

Wendy sat looking at Peter and was curious how old he was. So she asked him.

"I don't know," Peter replied uneasily, "but I am quite young. I ran away the day I was born. It was because I heard Father and Mother talking about what I would be when I became a man. I don't ever want to be a man. I want to stay a little boy and have fun forever. So I ran away to Kensington Gardens and lived a long time among the fairies."

Wendy gave him a look of admiration. Peter thought it was because he had run away, but Wendy was impressed that he knew fairies. So Peter told Wendy about fairies and how they began.

"You see, Wendy," said Peter, "when the first baby laughed for the first time, its laugh broke into a thousand pieces, and they all went skipping about. That was the beginning of fairies. And so there should be one fairy for every boy and girl."

"Isn't there?" Wendy asked.

"No," explained Peter. "Because every time a child says, 'I don't believe in fairies,' there is a fairy somewhere that falls down dead."

Now Peter thought he had talked enough about fairies. "I wonder where Tinker Bell has gone to," he said aloud.

4

Come Away, Come Away!

Wendy's heart fluttered with excitement. "Peter," she cried, clutching his arm, "do you mean that there is a fairy in this room?"

"She was here a moment ago," he replied. "You don't hear her, do you?"

"The only sound I hear," said Wendy, "is a tinkle of bells."

"Well, that's Tink—that's the fairy language."

The sound came from the chest of drawers, and Peter smiled a wide grin. No one could look quite as merry as Peter. He had the loveliest of gurgles for a laugh—he still had his first baby laugh.

"I think I shut her up in the drawer!" cried Peter gleefully. When he let poor Tink out, she flew around the room, screaming with fury.

"I'm very sorry," Peter said. "I didn't know you were in there. Tink, I think this lady wishes you were her fairy."

Tinker Bell answered in a nasty tone, and Peter had

to apologize for her. "Tink is not polite," said Peter. "She says she would never be your fairy."

But Wendy was not offended. She was too busy wondering all about Peter. "Where do you live now?" she asked.

"With the lost boys," Peter answered. "They are children who fall out of their strollers when their nurses are looking the other way. If they are not claimed in seven days by their parents, they are sent far away to Neverland. I'm captain."

"Oh, what fun it must be!" cried Wendy.

"Yes," said Peter slyly, "but we are rather lonely. We have no female friends."

"But none of the others are girls?" Wendy asked.

"Oh, no," said Peter. "Girls are much too clever to fall out of their strollers."

This flattered Wendy very much. "You may give me a kiss," she said to Peter. For a moment, she had forgotten that Peter thought a thimble was a kiss.

"I thought you would want it back," Peter said a little angrily and offered to return the thimble.

"Oh," said Wendy. "I don't mean a kiss. I mean a thimble."

"What's that?" asked Peter.

"It's like this," she said. And she kissed him.

"Funny!" Peter said. "Now shall I give you a thimble?"

"If you wish," she said. Peter thimbled her and almost immediately, Wendy shrieked.

"What is it, Wendy?" Peter asked.

"I felt as if someone was pulling my hair," Wendy said.

"That must be Tink," said Peter. "I never knew her to be so naughty before."

Tink was darting around again and seemed very angry.

"Wendy, Tink says she will do that to you every time I give you a thimble."

Peter went back to explaining why the lost boys would want a girl in Neverland. "You see, I don't know any stories," continued Peter. "None of the lost boys know any."

"How perfectly awful," said Wendy.

"Your mother was telling you such a lovely story the other night," said Peter, "about the prince who couldn't find the lady with the glass slipper."

"Oh, that was Cinderella," Wendy said. "The prince found her and they lived happily ever after."

Peter was so glad that he rose from the floor. "Where are you going?" Wendy asked.

"To tell the other boys."

"Don't go," said Wendy. "I know lots of stories." So Peter came back with a greedy look in his eyes. This should have alarmed Wendy, but it didn't. "Oh, I could tell stories to the other boys," she said.

Peter gripped Wendy by the arm and began to pull her toward the window.

"Let me go!" she ordered.

"Wendy, come with me!" said Peter.

Of course, Wendy was pleased to be asked, but she remembered her mother, and that she couldn't fly. Peter promised to teach her.

"We'll jump on the wind's back and away we'll go," cried Peter. "Neverland has mermaids with long tails."

"Oh, I wish I could see a mermaid," Wendy exclaimed.

Now Peter became very sly indeed. "Wendy, all the boys would think a lot of you. You could tuck us in at night. None of us has ever been tucked in."

"Oooo," said Wendy, and her arms went out to Peter. She could not resist. "Could you teach John and Michael to fly, too?"

"If you wish," Peter said casually.

So Wendy ran to John and Michael to wake them up. They rubbed their eyes and greeted Peter. But they realized that there was something wrong. Nana, who had been barking loudly, was quiet now. It was her silence that they noticed.

"Put out the light! Hide! Quick!" cried John. And so when their maid, Liza, entered the room with Nana, it was quiet and dark, and it seemed all was well in the nursery. One could even hear the children breathing as they slept. In fact, the children were hiding behind the curtains.

Liza was in a bad mood because she had been taken away from her cooking to come upstairs. Nana had begged her to.

"You see now that they are perfectly safe, don't you?" Liza said in frustration. "They are asleep in bed. Listen to their gentle breathing. There will be no more nonsense, Nana. If you bark again, I will go get Mr. and Mrs. Darling. And they will be very angry with you."

Liza tied Nana up again. But of course Nana continued to bark and finally broke free from her chain. In a moment, she burst into the dining room of the neighbors' house at Number 27 and put her paws in the air. Mr. and Mrs. Darling knew at once that something terrible had happened. They rushed out into the street toward home.

But by now it had been ten minutes since Nana had been in the nursery. Peter Pan can do a great deal in ten minutes.

In the nursery, Peter was teaching the children how to fly. It looked quite easy, but when they tried, the children went down instead of up. "How do you do it?" they asked.

"It's easy," Peter replied. "You just think lovely thoughts, and they lift you up into the air." But Peter had been fooling them. No one can fly without fairy dust. Fortunately, Peter had one hand covered with fairy dust, and he blew some at each of the children.

Peter told them just to let go. It was brave Michael who did it first, and he flew straight across the room. "I *flewed*!" he yelled.

Then John and Wendy let go as well. "Look at me!

Look at me!" they cried. Up and down they went, around and around.

"Hey, let's all go out!" cried John excitedly.

This is just what Peter had hoped would happen. Michael was ready, but Wendy wasn't so sure.

"Remember, there are mermaids," Peter said. "And pirates."

"Pirates!" cried John. "Let's go at once!"

It was just at this moment that Mr. and Mrs. Darling hurried toward the house with Nana. They looked up at the nursery window. Yes, it was still shut, but the room was ablaze with light. They could see the shadows on the curtain of three little figures in their pajamas circling around—not on the floor, but in the air.

And not three figures—four!

All trembling, they opened the front door. Mrs. Darling motioned for them to walk softly. Would they get to the nursery in time? They would have gotten there in time if it weren't for the stars again. They blew the window open, and the smallest star called out, "Come, Peter!"

Peter knew at once that there was not a moment to lose. "Come!" he then cried to the children. And he soared out into the night, followed by John, Michael, and Wendy.

Mr. and Mrs. Darling and Nana rushed into the nursery but they were too late. The children had flown away into the night sky.

5

The Flight

The children were delighted to be flying. They circled around church spires and other high buildings. They were over the sea when Wendy wondered how long they had been flying. John thought it was the second sea they'd flown over and that they were on their third night. Wendy wasn't sure and this worried her.

Sometimes it was dark, and sometimes light. Sometimes it was warm, and later cold. They were very sleepy, and that was a danger because the moment they dropped off to sleep, down they fell. The awful thing was that Peter thought this was funny.

"There he goes again!" he would cry gleefully as Michael suddenly dropped like a stone.

"Save him!" cried Wendy. Eventually Peter would dive through the air and catch Michael just before he hit the sea. But he always waited until the last moment.

Peter, however, could sleep in the air without falling. He would lie on his back and float.

"You must be more polite to him," Wendy whispered to John when they were playing Follow the Leader.

"Then tell him to stop showing off," John said.

When playing Follow the Leader, Peter would fly close to the water and touch each shark's tail. The children could not touch the sharks half as well, and Peter knew this.

"But you must be nice to him," Wendy said again. "What would we do if he were to leave us?"

"We could go back," Michael said.

"But we could never find our way back without him," said Wendy. "And we don't even know how to stop."

Peter was not with them at the moment, and they felt a bit lonely up there by themselves. Peter could go so much faster than they could that he would suddenly shoot out of sight. While Peter was away, he would have adventures. He would return to them laughing over something funny he had said to a star. Or he would come back with mermaid scales still sticking to him.

After many moons, they did reach Neverland.

"There it is," Peter said calmly.

"Where, where?" the children cried.

It was strange that they all recognized the island at once. In fact, the island seemed like a familiar friend.

"John, there's the lagoon!"

"Look, Michael, there's your cave!"

"I see the smoke of the Indian camp!"

"Where? Show me, and I'll tell you by the way the smoke curls whether they are on the warpath."

Peter was a little annoyed with them for knowing so

much. In the old days, Neverland would become a little dark and scary at bedtime. One was quite glad the night-lights were on. It was even nice to hear Nana say that Neverland was all make-believe.

They had been flying apart, but now the children huddled close to Peter. His careless manner was gone and his eyes sparkled. "Would you like an adventure now?" he said calmly to John. "Or would you like to have your tea first?"

"What kind of adventure?" John asked carefully.

"There's a pirate asleep just beneath us," Peter told him. "If you like, I'll go down and kill him."

"Do you kill many pirates?" asked John.

"Tons," replied Peter.

John was impressed but decided to have tea first. He asked if there were many pirates on the island now. Peter said he had never known of so many. Then his face became very stern.

"Hook is captain now," he told them.

Michael began to cry and even John could only speak in gulps, for they knew of Hook and what a mean and terrible pirate he was.

"He was Blackbeard's bo'sun," John whispered. "He is the worst of them all. What is he like? Is he big?"

"Not as big as he once was," replied Peter. "I cut off his right hand. He has an iron hook in its place now. But he's still a good fighter because he uses the hook to claw with."

The children shivered with fear.

"There is one thing," Peter continued, "that every boy who serves me has to promise—and so must you."

John paled but said, "Aye, aye, sir."

"If we meet Hook in a fight, you must leave him for me," said Peter.

"I promise," said John loyally.

At the moment they were feeling less afraid because Tink was flying with them. In her light, they could see each other quite well. Then Tink said something to Peter in her twinkling fairy language.

"She tells me that the pirates sighted us and they've gotten Long Tom, their big gun, out. Of course, they probably saw her light. If they guess we are near it, they are sure to shoot."

The children gasped. "Tell Tink to go away!" all three cried.

But Peter refused. "She thinks we have lost our way," he said, "and she is frightened. I can't send her away by herself when she is frightened."

"Then tell her," Wendy begged, "to put out her light."

"She can't. That is the only thing fairies can't do," Peter explained.

Then John pulled out his hat. Tink agreed to travel in it if someone would carry it, and so it was settled. They flew on in silence now. It was the stillest silence they had ever known. Sometimes it was broken by a distant lapping sound, which Peter explained was the wild beasts drinking at the river.

A little later, they heard a rasping sound, which Peter said was the Indians sharpening their knives. When these noises stopped, the silence frightened them all.

Then the air was filled with a tremendous crash. The pirates had fired Long Tom at them. This is how the children learned the difference between an island of make-believe and the same island come true.

"Are you shot?" John whispered shakily.

"No," Michael said.

No one had been hit, but Peter had been carried away, far out to sea, by the wind of the shot. And Wendy was blown upward with Tinker Bell.

It would have been a good thing if Wendy had dropped the hat with Tinker Bell inside it. But she didn't know that Tink was about to lead her into grave danger—on purpose.

Tink was not always all bad—sometimes she was good. Fairies have to be all bad or all good. Because they are so small, they have room for only one feeling at a time.

At the moment, Tink was very jealous of Wendy. But Wendy did not know this, and Tink's lovely tinkle of talk sounded to Wendy as if she said, "Follow me and all will be well."

Wendy called to Peter, John, and Michael, but got no answer. And since she did not know that Tink did not like her, Wendy followed Tink into danger.

6

The Island Come True

As Peter was on his way back, Neverland woke into life. Everything is usually quiet on the island when Peter is away. But since Peter does not allow laziness, the island comes alive when he returns.

On this evening, the lost boys were out looking for Peter, the pirates were out looking for the lost boys, the Indians were out looking for the pirates, and the beasts were out looking for the Indians. They were going around and around the island in a large circle, but they did not meet because they were all traveling at the same rate. All wanted blood except for the boys, who were out to greet Peter tonight.

The number of lost boys on the island varied from time to time. When they seemed to be growing up, Peter got rid of them. But at this time, there were six of them. The first to pass was Tootles, who had been in the fewest adventures. He seemed to just miss the action by a few minutes every time. Tootles was the most humble of them all.

Next came Nibs, who was happy and suave, followed by Slightly, who danced to his own music. Slightly thought the most of himself. Curly came fourth. He was the one who always admitted to Peter that he had done something wrong, even if he hadn't. Last came the twins.

The boys vanished into the darkness. After a little while, the pirates followed along their track. We can hear them before they are seen because they are singing a dreadful song. There was never a more villainous-looking bunch of men. There was Cecco, the Italian, and Bill Jukes, who was tattooed over every inch of his body. Then came Cookson, Starkey, and Skylights. The Irish bo'sun Smee, Noodler, Mullins, and Alf Mason came behind them.

In the middle of the men was the feared James Hook. He lay in a kind of chariot pulled by his men. And in place of his right hand, he had an iron hook. This terrible man treated his men as dogs, and they obeyed him. His hair was dark with long black curls. He was capable of being polite—he had been brought up well. But he certainly didn't act well toward others.

It was said that Hook had great courage. The only thing he was afraid of was the sight of his own blood. The scariest part of him, no doubt, was his iron claw.

Now the Indians were on the pirates' trail. They were creeping noiselessly down the warpath. They carried tomahawks and knives, and their chests gleamed with paint. Out in front was Great Big Little Panther, a very brave Indian. Bringing up the rear was Tiger Lily, a princess of the Indians, who was quite beautiful.

Soon the Indians' place was taken by the beasts that were coming behind them. Lions, tigers, bears, and the smaller beasts traveled with their tongues hanging out. They were hungry that night.

When they had passed, the last figure walked by—a giant crocodile.

Soon the boys appeared again. All were on a sharp lookout in front. None suspected that danger might be creeping up behind them.

The first group to fall out of the moving circle was the boys. "I do wish Peter would come back," someone said nervously. "I would like to hear more about Cinderella."

They talked of Cinderella, and Tootles thought his mother must have been just like her. It was only when Peter was away that they talked of their mothers, since Peter didn't allow it.

While they talked, the boys heard a distant sound. It was the grim song of the pirates. Instantly the lost boys disappeared. Rabbits could not have vanished so quickly. The boys had already slipped into their home underground. There is no entrance to be seen, but if you look closely, there are seven large trees. Each has a hole in its hollow trunk as large as a boy. These are the seven entrances to their home underground—the very home Hook had been seeking for a long time.

As the pirates came nearer, the quick eye of Starkey saw Nibs disappear through the woods. At once he pulled out his pistol, but Hook gripped his shoulder.

"Put the pistol back," Hook said in a low voice.

"It was one of the lost boys," replied Starkey.

"Aye, but your pistol will bring the Indians on us," said Hook.

"Shall I go after him, Captain?" asked Smee eagerly.

"No," said Hook darkly. "He is only one, and I want all seven. Split up and look for them." So the pirates disappeared among the trees.

Hook was left talking to Smee. "Most of all," Hook said passionately, "I want their captain, Peter Pan. 'Twas he who cut off my arm." Hook held up his hook angrily. "I've waited a long time to shake his hand with this!" he called out. Then he looked at his hook and frowned. "Peter flung my arm to a crocodile passing by."

"I have noticed your fear of crocodiles," Smee said.

"It liked my arm so much that it has followed me ever since—licking its lips for the rest of me."

"In a way, it's a sort of compliment," said Smee.

"I want no such compliments," barked Hook. "I want Peter Pan." Then he sat down on a large mushroom and sighed. "That crocodile would have had me long ago, except that it swallowed a clock that ticks inside it. I can hear it, and before the crocodile can reach me, I take off."

"Someday the clock will break down, and he will get you," Smee noted.

"Aye," said Hook. "That is the fear that haunts me."

Suddenly Hook felt very warm. He jumped up. "It's hot!" he said of his backside. They examined the mushroom and pulled it up easily. Smoke began to come out of it.

"A chimney!" they both said at once. They had discovered the chimney of the boys' underground home.

And not only smoke came out of it. They heard children's voices. The boys felt so safe in their home that they were happily chattering. The pirates looked around and discovered the seven holes in the seven trees.

Hook stood in thought for several moments. Then a smile curled his lips. "Those silly boys didn't know that they did not need a door for each of them. That shows they have no mother."

Just as Hook and Smee began to sing their pirate song, another sound interrupted them and made them stand suddenly still.

Tick tick tick tick!

Hook shuddered. "The crocodile!" he gasped and dashed off.

Indeed it was the crocodile. It had passed the Indians, who were on the trail of the pirates. It kept on Hook's trail, and the pirates left with Hook.

Soon the boys came out of their home. Nibs spoke up. "I have seen a great white bird flying this way," he said. "It looks so tired."

"It's coming!" said Curly, pointing at Wendy in the sky.

Wendy was almost overhead, and they could hear Tinker Bell. The jealous fairy was now plainly mean to

Wendy. She was darting at her from every direction, pinching her fiercely.

"Peter wants you to shoot the Wendy," Tink called to the boys.

"Let us do what Peter wishes," replied the simple boys. They rarely asked questions about his orders. "Quick, bows and arrows!"

Tootles pulled out his weapon and aimed.

"Hurry, Tootles!" screamed Tink. "Peter will be so pleased."

"Out of the way," he called to Tink. Then he fired.

In the next moment, Wendy fluttered to the ground with an arrow in her chest.

7

The Wendy Bird

"I have shot the Wendy," Tootles said proudly. "Peter will be so pleased with me."

Overhead, Tinker Bell rushed into hiding without being noticed. The boys crowded around Wendy, and as they looked, a terrible quiet fell over them.

Slightly was the first to speak. "This is no bird," he said in a scared voice. "I think it is a lady."

"A lady?" cried Tootles, trembling.

"And we have killed her," Nibs said hoarsely.

They all whipped off their caps and held them to their chests in a show of respect.

"Now I see that Peter was bringing us a lady to take care of us at last!" said Curly.

"And you have killed her!" said one of the twins.

They were very sorry for themselves, and when Tootles took a step closer to the rest of the boys, they turned from him.

Tootles' face went white. "I've wanted a mother for so long. But when at last she came, I killed her." He moved slowly away from the group. "I'm afraid of Peter now."

It was at this moment that they heard Peter call

out to them. He crowed his usual crow when he returned to Neverland.

"Peter!" all of the lost boys called in return. Then, "Hide her!" they said of Wendy, and they gathered quickly around her.

"Greetings, boys," Peter said as he dropped in front of them. They saluted and then there was silence.

Peter frowned. "I am back," he said shortly. "Why aren't you cheering?" The boys opened their mouths to reply, but they could say nothing.

"Great news, boys," Peter continued. "I've brought a mother for you all." Still there was no sound except for the thud of Tootles, who had dropped to his knees.

"Haven't you seen her?" Peter asked. "She flew this way."

"Peter," Tootles said quietly, "I will show her to you. Move back, boys."

They all stood back so Peter could see. After he had looked at Wendy for a while, Peter said uncomfortably, "She is dead." Then he saw the arrow sticking out of her chest.

Peter removed it and asked sternly, "Whose arrow is this?"

"Mine," Tootles replied, still on his knees.

Peter raised his hand with the arrow, ready to hurt Tootles. But he stopped. "I cannot do it," he said finally, and he put down the arrow.

The boys looked at Peter in surprise. But Nibs was

looking at Wendy. "The Wendy lady raised her arm!" he said. He bent down and listened closely to Wendy's whispers. "I think she said, 'Poor Tootles,'" Nibs declared.

"The Wendy lady lives," cried Slightly.

Peter knelt beside Wendy and found his acorn button around her neck.

"See," said Peter, "the arrow struck this. It is the kiss I gave her. It has saved her life."

"I remember kisses," said Slightly knowingly. "Let me see it. Aye, that's a kiss all right."

Overhead came a wailing voice. "It is Tinker Bell," said Curly. "She is crying because Wendy lives."

Then the boys told Peter of Tink's crime. They had never seen Peter look so stern.

"Tinker Bell," he cried. "I am your friend no more. Begone forever." Tink flew onto his shoulder and pleaded with him. But Peter brushed her off.

Wendy raised her arm again in protest. So Peter said, "Well, begone for a whole week then, Tink."

8

The Little House

The boys discussed what to do with Wendy. "Let us carry her down into the house," Curly suggested.

"I don't think we should move her," said Peter.

"Let's build a little house around her," suggested Peter. They were all delighted at this idea. In a moment, the boys were busy scurrying this way and that. They were looking for bedding, and wood for a fire.

Meanwhile, John and Michael appeared, dragging themselves along. They fell asleep standing, and then woke up, and moved another step before falling asleep again.

John and Michael were quite relieved to find Peter. But Peter barely noticed them since he was busy measuring Wendy's feet to see how large a house they would need to build.

"Is Wendy asleep?" Michael and John asked.

"Yes," replied the lost boys together.

"What are you all doing?" Michael and John wondered aloud.

"Building a house for the Wendy," came the reply.

"For Wendy?" said John with surprise. "But she is only a girl!"

"That," explained Curly, "is why we are her servants."

"You are Wendy's servants?" cried John.

"Yes, and you are, too," said Peter calmly, and returned to his work. "Slightly," called Peter, "get a doctor."

"Aye, aye," said Slightly at once. He disappeared, scratching his head and wondering what to do. He knew Peter must be obeyed, but he didn't know any doctors. So Slightly returned in a few moments wearing John's hat and looking very serious as he approached Peter.

"Please, sir," said Peter to Slightly. "Are you a doctor?"

"Yes," replied Slightly anxiously.

The big difference between Peter and the other boys was that they knew when something was make-believe and Peter did not. This troubled the boys sometimes—especially when they had to make-believe that they had eaten dinner.

"Sir, the lady is very ill," explained Peter. "Will you help her?"

"I will put a glass thing in her mouth," said Slightly to explain what he was doing. He made-believe this part while Peter waited.

"How is she?" asked Peter.

"Oh, this has cured her," said Slightly the doctor.

"I am so glad!" cried Peter. And the doctor went away.

"If we only knew what kind of house she would like to have," said one of the boys.

"Her mouth is opening," said another boy.

"Perhaps she is going to sing us her answer," said Peter. "Wendy, sing what kind of house you would like to have."

Immediately, without opening her eyes, Wendy began to sing:

"I wish I had a pretty house,
The littlest ever seen,
With funny little red walls
And roof of mossy green."

The boys were thrilled to hear this because the branches they had collected were red with sap and all of the ground was covered with green moss. Then Wendy sang a bit more:

"Oh, really next I think I'll have
Gay windows all about,
With roses peeping in, you know,
And babies peeping out."

With blows from their fists, the lost boys made windows in the little house. Large yellow leaves were the curtains. But roses?

"Yes, roses," said Peter sternly.

Quickly they made-believe to grow the loveliest roses up the walls. They hoped Peter wouldn't order babies.

The house was quite beautiful, and Wendy was cozy within it. Peter strode up and down beside the house, ordering finishing touches.

Now the house was truly finished. There was nothing left to do but knock. "All look your best," Peter called out to the boys. "First impressions are awfully important."

He was glad no one asked him what first impressions were, since he did not know. The boys were all too busy looking their best, anyway.

Peter knocked politely. The boys were wondering, *Would anyone answer the knock? If she did, what would she be like?*

The door opened and a lady came out. All the boys whipped off their hats. Wendy looked properly surprised, and this was just what they had hoped.

"Wendy lady," said Slightly first. "We built this house for you."

"Oh, say you're pleased," cried Nibs.

"It's a lovely, darling house," replied Wendy. And they were the very words they hoped she would say.

"And we are your children," cried the twins.

Then the boys went down on their knees, held out their arms, and said, "Oh, Wendy lady, be our mother."

"Ought I?" asked Wendy. "But I am only a girl. I have no real experience."

"That doesn't matter," said Peter, who knew the least about mothers. "What we need is just a nice motherly person."

"Oh, well," said Wendy. "I feel that is exactly what I am."

"Yes, it is," they all cried. "We saw it at once."

"Very well," Wendy said. "I will do my best. Come inside, children. Before I put you to bed, we can finish the story of Cinderella."

So in they went. It's a mystery how they all fit in that tiny house, but you can squeeze very tightly in Neverland. And that was the first of many joyous evenings they had with Wendy. A little later, she tucked the boys into the great bed in their home under the trees. She herself slept in the little house, and Peter kept watch with his sword ready. The pirates and the wolves could be heard in the distance.

9

The Home Under the Ground

One of the first things Peter did the next day was to measure Wendy, John, and Michael for hollow trees. They would each have their own entrance to the underground home like the lost boys. Peter measured them for their trees as carefully as a tailor.

Soon they all loved that home under the ground, especially Wendy. There was an enormous fireplace and a bed that filled the room. All the boys slept in it, except Michael. Wendy insisted that since he was the littlest, he had to be the baby in the household. So Michael slept in a basket that hung from the ceiling.

It was a simple home, something like a bears' den. There was one small recess in the wall, which was Tinker Bell's private apartment. It was beautiful and it was closed off by a tiny curtain. Tinker Bell did not like the rest of the house that the others occupied.

All those boys gave Wendy quite a lot to do in their underground home. Her favorite time was in the evening when the boys had gone to bed, and she could have a few moments to herself.

As the days went by, did Wendy think much about her parents she had left behind? This is difficult to say because time in Neverland is quite different than real time. Wendy did not really worry about her mother and father, though. She was sure they would keep the window open for them to fly back through.

Wendy did worry, though, that her brothers were beginning to forget about their parents. John remembered his parents as people he once knew, but Michael was quite willing to believe that Wendy was his real mother. This scared Wendy a bit. She would sometimes quiz them to see what they could remember—such as what color Mother's eyes are. Wendy, you see, had been forgetting, too.

Just about every day, Peter went out on adventures. Sometimes he would come home with his head bandaged, and Wendy would fuss over him. Sometimes he would tell a dazzling tale of what had happened, and sometimes Peter would forget and not say a word.

There were so many adventures that it would be impossible to tell about all of them here. There was a battle with the Indians at Slightly Gulch. That was especially interesting because in the middle of the fight, Peter suddenly changed sides.

He called out, "I'm an Indian today! What are you, Tootles?"

And Tootles answered, "Indian. What are you, Nibs?" And Nibs said, "Indian. What are you, Twin?" And on it went until all the lost boys said they were

Indians. Of course, this would have ended the fight if the Indians had not agreed to change sides and be lost boys, which the Indians did at once. So they all began fighting again.

Another adventure happened when the pirates made a poisoned cake. They had placed pieces of it in clever places around the island for the lost boys to eat. But Wendy always snatched the pieces away from the hands of her children before they put any of them in their mouths.

There are so many other stories to be told, but there isn't room for them here. One story must be told, though—the adventure at the Mermaids' Lagoon.

10

The Mermaids' Lagoon

The children often spent long days at the lagoon, swimming and playing mermaid games in the water. Wendy was disappointed to discover that mermaids are not at all friendly. As soon as Wendy got near a mermaid, the mermaid would swim away. The mermaids treated everyone the same way, except Peter. They would talk with Peter on Marooners' Rock by the hour.

The children liked to rest on that rock in the lagoon. Wendy insisted that the boys rest every day after lunch. One day, the boys were all dozing on Marooners' Rock while Wendy was doing some stitching next to them.

Suddenly something changed on the lagoon. The sun went away, and turned the water cold. When Wendy looked up, she saw that the sunny lagoon now looked quite dark and unfriendly. She knew that night had not arrived but that something as dark as night had come. What was it?

Of course, she should have awakened the children at once. But since she was a young and inexperienced mother, she did not. She heard a muffled sound of a boat's oars in the water. Wendy was very afraid.

Luckily there was one person among them who could sniff out danger even in his sleep. Peter awoke and jumped up, wide-awake. With one warning cry, he woke the others. He stood motionless, with one hand to his ear. "Pirates!" he cried. A strange smile crossed his face, and Wendy shuddered.

"Dive!" called Peter.

The boat came nearer to Marooners' Rock. It was the pirate dinghy, with three people in it: Smee, Starkey, and Tiger Lily. The pirates had caught Tiger Lily boarding their ship with a big knife. Her hands and feet were tied, and she knew what was about to happen to her. She was going to be left on the rock to die.

In the past, evil captains had put sailors on Marooners' Rock to drown. Because when the tide rose, the rock would be underwater.

"Here's the rock," said Smee. "Now all we have to do is hoist her onto it and leave her there."

Quite near the rock but out of sight were Peter and Wendy bobbing in the water. Wendy was crying, for this was the first terrible thing she had ever seen. Peter decided he would save Tiger Lily. The easiest way would have been to wait until the pirates were gone. But Peter never chose the easiest way to do anything.

Peter imitated the voice of Captain Hook. "Ahoy there, you lubbers!" he called out. His voice sounded just like Hook's voice.

"The captain!" the pirates cried, staring at each

other in surprise. "We are putting the Indian on the rock!" called Smee.

"Set her free!" came the surprising answer.

"What? Free?" exclaimed the pirates.

"Yes, untie her hands and let her go," said Peter.

"But, Captain—"

"At once," said Peter, "or you'll have to deal with me!"

"This is very strange," gasped Smee.

"We'd better do what the captain ordered," said Starkey nervously.

"Aye, aye," agreed Smee, and he untied Tiger Lily's hands. At once, she slid into the water as quickly as an eel and was gone.

11

The Meeting

Wendy was very pleased by Peter's cleverness. However, she had only a moment to rejoice over Tiger Lily's release before they heard something else.

"Boat, ahoy!" rang out Captain Hook's voice over the lagoon. But this time it was not Peter who had spoken. It was the real Captain Hook. And he was also in the water.

Hook swam to the boat and pulled himself up into it.

"Captain, all is well?" asked Starkey.

Captain Hook did not answer immediately. He let out a long sigh. "The game's up," he said finally. "Those boys have found a mother."

Though she was frightened, Wendy glowed with pride.

"Oh, evil day!" cried Starkey.

"What's a mother?" said Smee.

Wendy was so shocked that she forgot to be quiet. "He doesn't know!" she exclaimed. Peter pulled her under the water to quiet her.

"What was that?" said Hook.

"I heard nothing," Starkey replied. He held his

lantern up just to be sure. When they looked, they saw a strange sight. It was a Never bird sitting on her nest—and the nest was floating in the water.

"See," said Hook, answering Smee's question, "that is a mother. The nest must have fallen into the water. But a mother wouldn't desert her children. She stays with them always."

For a moment, Hook's voice broke as he remembered his childhood days. He brushed away a tear with his hook.

"If she is a mother," said Starkey, "perhaps she is here to help Peter Pan."

Hook winced. "Aye, that's what I'm afraid of."

Then Smee had an idea. "Maybe we could capture the boys' mother and make her *our* mother."

"It is a good scheme," replied Hook. "We could capture the children and carry them to the boat. We can make the boys walk the plank, and Wendy can be our mother."

Again Wendy forgot to be quiet. "Never!" she cried.

"What was that?" said Hook again.

But they could see nothing. "Do you agree?" Hook asked them.

"Yes!" the pirates said together.

Then Hook remembered Tiger Lily. "Where is the Indian?" he demanded suddenly.

Hook was playful and sometimes joked with the pirates. Smee and Starkey thought he was joking now.

"We let her go," they answered calmly.

"Let her go?" cried Hook.

"They were your orders," they replied.

Hook's face went black with rage, but he saw that the pirates believed their words. "Lads," he said in a shaky voice, "I gave no such order."

Then he turned out toward the lagoon and said, "Spirit that haunts the lagoon tonight, do you hear me?"

Of course, Peter should have kept quiet. But he didn't. He said in Hook's voice, "Odds, bobs, hammer, and tongs, I hear you."

Smee and Starkey clung to each other in terror.

"Who are you?" Hook asked carefully.

"I am James Hook," said the voice, "captain of the *Jolly Roger*."

"You are not," said Hook. "If you are Hook, tell me who I am."

"A codfish," replied the voice.

"A codfish!" Hook echoed angrily. It was then that his pride was wounded. He could see his men move away from him.

"We have been captained by a codfish all this time," they muttered. "This is not good."

"Hook," the captain called out to the lagoon, "do you have another voice?"

The trouble was that Peter could never resist a game. And so he answered in his own voice, "I have."

"And another name?" asked the true Hook.

"Aye, aye," said Peter.

"Animal?"

"No."

"Man?"

"No."

"Boy?"

"Yes. Do you give up?" asked Peter. He was carrying this game too far, and the pirates saw their chance.

"Yes, yes," the pirates answered eagerly.

"I am Peter Pan!" he cried.

In a moment, Hook was himself again. "Now we have him," Hook shouted. "Into the water, Smee! Take him dead or alive!"

Then came the voice of Peter. "Are you ready, boys?"

"Aye, aye," came the voices from around the lagoon where the boys had been hiding.

"Then get those pirates!" Peter called out to them.

The fight was short and sharp. John climbed into the boat to get Starkey, but he wriggled overboard. There were yelps and cries all over the lagoon.

All this time, Peter was looking for Hook. The two did not meet in the water. Hook climbed on the rock to catch his breath, and at the same moment, Peter crawled up the opposite side of the same rock.

Neither knew that the other was coming. Their hands met as they gripped the rock, climbing out of the water. When they raised their heads, their faces were almost touching.

Peter had a feeling of gladness when he met Hook. Quickly he grabbed Hook's knife from his belt and was about to kill him when he saw that he was higher on the rock than Hook. This gave Peter an advantage, and it would not be fighting fair. So Peter gave Hook a hand up.

It was then that Hook bit him. Peter could only stare in shock from the unfairness of the bite. Twice Hook's iron claw struck Peter.

Then, minutes later, the boys saw Hook swimming wildly for the ship with a face white with fear. Chasing after Hook was the crocodile.

12

The Never Bird

Normally the boys would have cheered at the sight of the crocodile chasing Hook, but they were worried and were looking for Peter and Wendy. When they stopped calling their names for a moment, the boys heard only silence.

They did not know that Wendy and Peter had just gotten themselves out of the water and up on Marooners' Rock. Wendy had fainted and Peter was lying beside her. Peter knew that the water was rising and that they would soon be drowned, but he was hurt and tired and could do nothing about it.

After Wendy woke, Peter quickly explained the situation. "I can't help you, Wendy," Peter moaned. "Hook wounded me. I can neither fly nor swim."

"Do you mean that we will be drowned?" cried Wendy.

"Look how the water is rising," Peter answered.

While they lay there in misery, something brushed against Peter's cheek. It was the tail of a kite, which Michael had made a few days before. "It lifted Michael into the air," cried Peter. "It could carry you!"

Wendy insisted that Peter go, but he would not hear of it. Already he was tying the tail around her. Wendy refused to go without him, but Peter pushed her from the rock and said good-bye. In a few minutes, Wendy was out of sight and Peter was alone on the lagoon.

The rock was quite small now, and it would soon be underwater. Peter could hear the mermaids calling to the moon. For once, Peter was afraid.

But the next moment, he was standing on the rock with a smile on his face. *To die will be an awfully big adventure*, thought Peter.

As Peter heard the mermaids closing the doors to their bedrooms under the sea, the waters rose until they were nibbling at his feet. Peter watched the only moving thing on the lagoon to pass the time. At first he thought it was a piece of paper. Then he noticed it was coming toward him—against the tide.

It was the Never bird. She was trying very hard to reach Peter as she sat on her nest. She hopped up and pushed the nest toward the rock with all her might. The bird wanted Peter to get into the nest and drift ashore. She had come to save him! Then she flew into the air.

Peter grabbed the nest. Of course, there were still eggs in it. So he decided to put them in his hat and let them float on the lagoon. The Never bird cawed her thanks to Peter when she saw what he had done.

When Peter finally reached the lost boys' home underground, he was greeted with great whoops of joy. Wendy, who had been carried all over the island by the kite, had arrived home safely, too. Every boy had adventures to tell, but the biggest adventure of all was that they were several hours late for bed. The boys tried to stay up even longer by demanding bandages. Even though Wendy was happy and relieved to have them all home again, she insisted the boys go straight to bed.

13

The Happy Home

After the battle with the pirates at the lagoon, the Indians became the lost boys' friends. Peter had saved Tiger Lily, and now the Indians would do anything to please him. All night, the Indians would sit aboveground, keeping watch over the lost boys' home in case the pirates attacked again.

This night, the boys were having their dinner down below. Peter was the only one missing. He had gone out to get the time. The only way to find out what time it was on the island was to find the crocodile and then stay near him until the clock struck the hour.

While Wendy sewed by the fire that night, the boys played around her. It was a group of happy faces and dancing limbs, and it was a familiar scene in this home. But we are seeing it for the last time. Much later, the lost boys named this evening the Night of Nights.

Wendy heard a noise and was first to recognize it. "Children, I hear your father's step. He likes you to meet him at the door."

The first twin went to Peter. "Father, we want to dance with you." Peter was the best dancer among the group, but he pretended he wasn't.

"Me? My old bones would rattle," he said with a smile.

The children went to put on their pajamas while Wendy and Peter sat by the fire. "Ah, there is nothing more pleasant than to spend an evening by the fire with the little ones nearby," Peter exclaimed.

"It is sweet, isn't it?" Wendy said. "Peter, I think Curly has your nose."

"And Michael takes after you," Peter noted.

Peter stared blankly at Wendy for a minute. Wendy noticed he was deep in thought. "Peter, what is it?"

"I was just thinking," he said. "It is only make-believe, isn't it, that I am their father?"

"Oh, yes," said Wendy.

"Because it would make me seem so old if I were their real father," worried Peter.

"But they are ours, Peter, yours and mine," she said.

"But not really?" he answered.

"Not if you don't wish it," Wendy replied. And she heard his sigh of relief.

In the next hour, which turned out to be their last hour together in their home, the children sang and danced in their pajamas. They told stories before it was time for Wendy's final good-night story.

They all climbed into bed, and Wendy began. It was the story the children loved best but the one that Peter hated. Usually when Wendy began to tell this story, he left the room or put his hands over his ears. But tonight Peter stayed and listened.

14

Wendy's Story

"There was once a gentleman and a lady," Wendy said as she settled down to tell her story. "Mr. Darling was the gentleman's name and the lady's name was Mrs. Darling."

"I knew them," John said.

"I think I knew them," said Michael doubtfully.

"They had three children," Wendy continued, "and the children had a nurse called Nana. But Mr. Darling got angry with her and put her in the yard, and so all the children flew away."

"It's an awfully good story," interrupted Nibs.

"They flew away to Neverland," said Wendy, "where the lost children are."

"Oh, Wendy," cried Tootles. "Was one of the lost children called Tootles?"

"Yes, he was," she replied.

"I am in a story! Hooray!" he cried.

"Hush now," said Wendy. "Think about the feelings of the unhappy parents with all of their children flown away."

"Ooohh," they all moaned. "Think of the empty beds."

"It's awfully sad," said the first twin.

"I don't see how it can have a happy ending," said the second twin.

"If you knew how great a mother's love is," Wendy told them, "you would have no fear." Now she came to the part that Peter hated.

"You see," Wendy went on, "the girl knew that her mother would always leave the window open for her children to fly back. So they stayed away for years and had a lovely time."

"Did they ever go back?" the boys asked.

"Let us take a peek into the future," said Wendy. And they all tried very hard to do just that. "Years have rolled by, and who is that elegant lady at London Station?" she asked.

"Can it be—it is the fair Wendy!"

"And who are the two noble figures with her?" she asked. "Now they are grown-up men. Can they be John and Michael? They are!

"See," she went on, "there is the window still open. So up they went to their mommy and daddy. I cannot describe how happy they were to see their children home."

That was the story, and the boys were pleased with it. And so was the storyteller. But one person was not happy. It was Peter—and he gave a hollow-sounding groan.

"What is it, Peter?" cried Wendy, running to him. She thought he was sick. Wendy felt his chest.

"It isn't that kind of pain," Peter replied darkly.

"Then what kind is it?" she asked.

"Wendy, you are wrong about mothers," he said.

All the children gathered around Peter to hear what he had to say. He slowly told them what he had been keeping from them.

"Long ago," he started, "I thought that my mother would always keep a window open for me, so I stayed away for moons and moons. But when I flew back, the windows were locked. My mother had forgotten me, and there was another little boy sleeping in my bed."

This might not have been true, but Peter thought it was true. And it scared them all.

"Are you sure mothers are like that?" they asked.

"Yes," he replied.

"Wendy, let's go home!" cried John and Michael together.

"Yes," she said, clutching her brothers.

"Tonight?" asked the lost boys.

"Yes, at once," cried Wendy with determination. She had become worried that her mother was mourning them. She was so worried that she did not think of Peter's feelings at that moment.

"Peter, will you make plans for us to go?" she asked.

"If you wish it," he said coolly.

But of course, Peter cared very much. And he did not care for grown-ups at all, who, as usual, were spoiling everything.

15

Peter Won't Go

After making some preparations, Peter returned to their underground home. The lost boys were in a panic at the thought of losing Wendy, and they were devising a plan to keep her.

"We won't let her go," they cried.

"Let's keep her prisoner."

"Aye, chain her up."

Then Peter returned and set things straight. They would not keep Wendy in Neverland against her will. Peter spoke to Wendy about the trip. "I have asked the Indians to guide you through the wood. Then Tinker Bell will take you across the sea."

"Thank you," Wendy said to Peter.

Of course, Tink was delighted that Wendy was leaving. In the meantime, the boys looked sadly at Wendy as she packed for the journey.

"Dear ones," Wendy said, "if you will come with me, I think I could get my father and mother to adopt you."

The boys jumped for joy. "But won't they think we are a handful?" cried Nibs in the middle of his jump.

"Oh, no," said Wendy, thinking quickly. "It will mean we have to put a few beds in the living room, though."

"Peter, can we go?" they all asked at once.

"All right," Peter said.

"Then get your things," Wendy said to Peter, hoping he was coming with them.

"I'm not going, Wendy," he said.

"Yes, Peter."

"No," he replied.

"But you could find your mother," pleaded Wendy.

Now, if Peter really did remember his mother, he never missed her. And he knew he did very well without one.

"No, no," he said to Wendy. "Perhaps she would say I was too old. And I just want to be a little boy forever."

"But, Peter—"

"No."

And so the others were told that Peter wasn't coming. When they heard the news, the boys stared at him with blank expressions.

"If you find your mothers," Peter said darkly, "I hope you will like them. Now, then, good-bye, Wendy." He held out his hand cheerily, as if they had to rush off and he had something important to do. Wendy had no choice but to take Peter's hand. She would have preferred a "thimble" from him instead.

"Will you remember to take your medicine, Peter?" Wendy asked.

"Yes," he replied.

That seemed to be everything. Then there was a long silence. Peter was not the type of boy to show his feelings in front of others.

"Are you ready, Tinker Bell?" he called.

"Aye, aye," she replied.

"Then lead the way," Peter told her.

Tink was about to lead the children home when the pirates made their terrible attack on the Indians. The air above their underground home was filled with shrieks, and the children could hear the sound of weapons clashing. The fighting sounded horrible.

Below, the boys stood still with their mouths open. Wendy fell on her knees, and all arms reached out for Peter. They all needed him now. As for Peter, he grabbed his sword. The desire for battle shone clearly in his eyes.

The pirate attack came as a complete surprise. At first, the Indians did not move a muscle. But a moment later, they grabbed their weapons and gave their war cry. However, it was too late.

Captain Hook must have felt joy at the pirates' win over the Indians, but he did not show it. He had not come out that night for the Indians. Hook wanted Peter Pan, Wendy, and the rest of the boys. But mostly he wanted Peter.

Peter was such a small boy that it's a wonder Hook

hated him so much. It's true that Peter threw his arm to the crocodile, but this was not what bothered Hook most. The truth was that Peter's pride disturbed Hook terribly. While Peter lived, Hook could not rest.

Now Wendy and the boys underground were listening carefully to the sounds outside. The fighting seemed to have stopped, and they knew that one side had won. But which side?

"If the Indians have won," said Peter, "they will beat the tom-tom drum. It is always their sign of victory."

Hook and the pirates were listening carefully at the entrances of the trees above. And they heard Peter's answer. Quickly Hook found the tom-tom and motioned for Smee to beat it. What a wicked idea!

After Smee beat the drum, the pirates listened for Peter again.

"The tom-tom," Peter cried. "An Indian victory!"

The children answered with a cheer that delighted the pirates above. As the pirates smirked at one another and rubbed their hands, Hook gave his orders: One man to each tree. The others form two lines.

16

The Children Are Carried Off

The first to come up a tree was Curly. He was passed from one pirate to another until he fell at the feet of Captain Hook. All the boys were plucked from their trees in this way.

Wendy was the last to come up her tree. When she was aboveground, Hook did not have her passed along as the others. With great politeness, he tipped his hat to her, offered his arm, and took her gently to the spot where the others were being tied up. Wendy was so fascinated by Hook's manners that she did not appear upset.

The pirates made sure the boys did not fly away by tying them up with ropes that were each the same length. When it was time to tie up Slightly, the rope wouldn't reach around him. He had grown much bigger than the other boys. After seeing this, Hook went to inspect Slightly's tree. He saw that Slightly had made his tree hole bigger so that he could fit through.

But the other boys did not know this. It was not safe to make one's tree hole bigger, since it meant that other, larger people could then get into their home. This was exactly what Hook had in mind.

When the captives were taken to his ship, Hook stayed behind. He tiptoed to Slightly's tree. He listened carefully for any sound from under the earth, but it was silent. *Is Peter Pan asleep,* thought Hook, *or is he waiting at the foot of Slightly's tree for me?* There was no way to know but to go down the tree and find out.

So down went Hook silently into the dark hole of the tree.

As his eyes got used to the dim light, Hook looked around and saw the great bed. On it lay Peter fast asleep.

Peter did not know that Wendy and the boys had been captured. After saying good-bye to them all and thinking they had left to go back to Wendy's parents, Peter had tried to pretend he didn't mind their leaving. He decided not to take his medicine, since that is exactly what Wendy had asked him to do. Then Peter lay down and fell asleep.

Hook stood silent at the foot of the tree and stared at his enemy. Peter looked so peaceful that Hook almost left him there and went back up the tree. Except for one thing—Peter's cockiness. Even in his sleep, Peter looked as if he thought a great deal of himself. And Hook couldn't ignore this.

As he looked around the room again, Hook noticed Peter's medicine bottle within his reach. He put his hand into his pocket and found a bottle of poison. It was a deadly potion that was strong enough to kill a grown man. Hook poured five drops of this poison into Peter's bottle and smiled an evil grin. With one last glance at Peter, Hook went back up the tree.

Much later, Peter awoke to a soft tapping. It was Tinker Bell.

"Let me in, Peter," she said excitedly. Her dress was covered with mud, and her face was flushed red.

"What is it?" he asked when he saw her.

Tink explained in a rush of words how Wendy and the boys were captured. Peter's heart raced as he listened.

"I'll rescue her!" cried Peter, and he leaped for his weapons. Then he thought of something he could do to please Wendy. He would take his medicine! His hand closed around the medicine bottle.

"No!" shrieked Tinker Bell, who had heard Hook muttering about his deadly deed as she raced through the forest to Peter.

"Why not?" he asked.

"It's poisoned," answered Tink.

"But who could have poisoned it?" Peter wondered aloud.

"Hook."

"Don't be silly," he said. "How could he have gotten down here?"

Tinker Bell could not explain, but she knew it was true. Peter did not believe her. He raised the bottle, and before it reached Peter's lips, Tink pushed in front of him and drank the liquid herself.

"Tink, how dare you drink my medicine?" cried Peter. But Tink did not answer, for she was already feeling faint from the poison. "Why, what's the matter, Tink?" Peter said, starting to panic.

"I've been poisoned," she replied softly. "And now I will die."

"Oh, Tink, did you drink it to save me?" he asked.

"Yes," said Tink in a whisper. She lay down, and her light was getting fainter. Peter knew that if the light went out, Tink would be gone.

Then Tink whispered in a low voice that she thought she could get well if children believed in fairies. There were no children in their home, but Peter addressed all of the children who might be dreaming in Neverland.

"Do you believe in fairies?" Peter cried. "If you believe, clap your hands. Don't let Tink die!"

Many clapped. Some didn't. A few clapped very loudly. But this was enough to save Tink. She sat up in bed. Her voice grew stronger and stronger, and then she popped up and was flashing around the room once more.

Peter was so very happy. But he still had Wendy and the lost boys to think about. "And now to rescue Wendy!" he shouted.

The moon was riding in a cloudy heaven when Peter rose from his tree with his weapons ready. As he headed for the ship, he made a promise to himself: "Hook or me this time."

17

The Pirate Ship

Close to the mouth of the pirate river stood the *Jolly Roger*. It was a dark and frightful-looking ship, and it fit the pirates who sailed it. Peter could see the men sprawled on the deck of the ship, playing cards and rolling dice.

Hook walked along the deck, deep in thought. He was quite pleased with himself at that moment. He thought that he had killed Peter with his poison, and he was proud to have all the lost boys on the ship, ready to walk the plank to their deaths.

"Are the children chained up so that they cannot fly away?" Hook asked his men.

"Aye, aye," came the reply.

"Then hoist them up," Hook said.

Except for Wendy, all of the prisoners were dragged from the hold below and were arranged in a line in front of Hook.

"Now then, bullies," began Hook. "Six of you will walk the plank tonight, but I have room for two cabin boys. Who will join me?"

Wendy had carefully instructed the boys earlier down below. "Be careful not to annoy Hook or upset him," she had said.

Tootles stepped forward politely. He hated the idea of joining such a horrible man. He thought it would be safest to blame someone else when giving his reason for not joining.

So Tootles explained carefully, "You see, sir, I don't think my mother would like me to be a pirate. Would your mother like you to be a pirate, Slightly?" he asked.

"I don't think so," Slightly responded. "Would your mother like you to be a pirate, Twin?" he asked.

"I don't think so," said the first twin. "Nibs, would your mo—"

"That's enough!" roared Hook. Then he looked over at John. "You, boy," Hook said to him. "You look as if you had a little pluck in you. Did you ever want to be a pirate, my hearty?"

John was surprised that Hook had singled him out. "I once thought of calling myself Red-handed Jack," he admitted.

"It's a good name," Hook said. "We'll call you that, if you join."

"What do you think, Michael?" John asked.

"What would you call me if I join?" Michael wanted to know.

"Blackbeard Joe."

Michael was naturally impressed. But he wanted John to decide if they should stay.

"Would we serve the King respectfully?" John asked Hook.

Hook clenched his teeth and answered, "You would

have to swear, 'Down with the King!'"

"Then we refuse," cried John.

"That seals your doom!" Hook roared. The angry pirates grabbed the boys. "Bring up their mother. Get the plank ready."

The boys' faces turned white as they watched Jukes and Cecco preparing the plank. But they tried to look brave when Wendy was brought up.

No words can tell how much Wendy hated the pirates. For the boys, there was some glamour in being a pirate, but Wendy saw none of this. She saw a dirty, evil ship that had not been cleaned in years. As the boys gathered around her, however, she thought only of them.

"So, my beauty," said Hook to Wendy in a syrupy sweet voice, "you will see your children walk the plank."

"Are they to die?" asked Wendy with such a nasty look at Hook that he almost fainted.

"They are," he snarled. "Silence everyone, for a mother's last words to her children."

At this moment, Wendy was grand. "I feel I have a message to you from your real mothers," she said, "and it is this: 'We hope our sons will die like English gentlemen.'"

Even the pirates were impressed. But Hook found his voice once more. "Tie her up!" he boomed.

It was Smee who tied Wendy to the mast. "See here, honey," he whispered to her, "I'll save you if you promise to be my mother."

"I would almost rather have no children at all," Wendy replied coldly.

Now all of the boys' eyes were on the plank, and they could only shiver as they stared at it. Hook took a step toward Wendy—but he never reached her.

Instead he heard the *tick-tick* of the crocodile and stopped in midstep.

They all heard it. Immediately all heads turned toward Hook. It was frightful to see the change that came over him at once. As if his bones had left his body, Hook fell over in a pile.

The *tick-tick* sound came steadily nearer. Then came the one thought that everyone had at the same time: The crocodile was about to board the ship. To try to get as far away from the sound as he could, Hook crawled on his knees along the deck.

"Hide me!" he cried hoarsely.

The pirates gathered around him. They had no thought of fighting the crocodile. That crocodile would find Hook at last. It was meant to be, it seemed.

While the pirates were busy hiding Hook, the lost boys became curious and rushed to the side of the boat to see the crocodile climbing in. But they got the strangest surprise.

For it was no crocodile coming to help them.

It was Peter.

He signaled to them not to say a word. Then Peter climbed into the ship and went on ticking.

18

"Hook or Me This Time"

As soon as Peter was on deck, he vanished into the cabin so he would not be seen. The pirates listened for the ticking once again.

"It's gone, Captain," Smee said to Hook. "All's still."

Slowly Hook let his head peek out of his collar, where he had tucked it in. He listened closely, but when he heard nothing, he drew himself up to his full height.

"Then here's to the plank!" Hook yelled. In order to frighten the prisoners more, he danced along the plank and, with an evil grin, sang a nasty song.

But while he was singing, there came a dreadful screech from the cabin. It wailed through the ship and died slowly away. Then there was a crowing sound, which was well understood by the boys to be Peter. But to the unknowing pirates, it was a frightening sound indeed.

"What was that?" cried Hook.

Pirate Bill Jukes teetered out of the cabin and fell over.

"What's the matter with him?" hissed Hook.

"He's dead," replied Cecco flatly.

"Bill Jukes is dead!" cried the startled pirates together.

"The cabin is as black as night," said Cecco, "but there is something terrible in there—the thing you heard crowing."

Hook could see the lost boys' happiness on their faces and the pirates lowering their heads. "Cecco," Hook said in a steely voice, "go in there and get me the crower."

Cecco was the bravest of the brave, but he refused to go. The captain raised his hook threateningly in front of Cecco. Finally the pirate gave in and walked to the cabin.

All was silent, and everyone listened closely. Again came the screech and then the crow.

"Who will get me the crower?" tried Hook again, looking around at his men. "I think I heard you volunteer, Starkey."

"No, by thunder!" he replied. "Have mercy, Captain."

But Hook held up his metal claw again. Starkey looked around for help, and when he found none, he backed up—and leaped off the plank into the sea.

"I guess I will have to go in there and bring out the crower myself!" cried Hook. He sped off to the cabin, holding his lantern. But Hook came staggering out a moment later without his lantern.

"Something blew out my light," he said in a shaky voice.

"Where is Cecco?" said one of the pirates.

"He's as dead as Jukes," Hook replied shortly.

"The ship is doomed!" cried one of the pirates.

The boys cheered at that. Hook swung around to look at them. He had almost forgotten the boys, but now he smiled an evil grin.

"Lads," Hook said to his crew, "put the boys in the cabin and let them fight the crower!"

And so the boys were driven in.

Wendy, who had been watching all along while she was tied to the mast, was waiting to see Peter again. She did not have long to wait. For, inside the cabin, Peter had found weapons for all of the lost boys. Then the boys quietly snuck out of the cabin and hid. Peter cut the rope that tied Wendy's hands to the mast. Of course, Peter and the lost boys could have flown away right then and been free. But Peter had made a promise that day: Hook or me this time. And he intended to keep that promise.

Once Wendy's hands were loose, Peter whispered for her to join the others in hiding. He took Wendy's place by the mast and put her cloak around him so that he would look like her. Then Peter took a deep breath and crowed.

Hearing that dreadful sound again, the pirates thought all the boys were now dead in the cabin. And they panicked. Hook could see that he was losing control of his men, so he tried to get the pirates to focus on something else.

"Throw the girl overboard," Hook cried. The pirates rushed at the cloaked figure on the mast.

"There's nothing that can save you now, missy," said Mullins.

"There is one," said the figure.

"What is that?" they all asked together.

"Peter Pan!" cried Peter as he flung off the cloak to show himself.

Then the pirates knew what had been lurking in the cabin. Twice Hook tried to speak, but he could not. In that terrible moment, perhaps his fierce heart broke.

"Go get them, boys!" yelled Peter.

There was a clash of weapons as the pirates and the lost boys fought all over the ship. Some pirates jumped overboard; some hid in the dark shadows of the boat. But the boys knew how to seek them out. It was a mighty battle, and the lost boys were winning.

Then suddenly Hook found himself face-to-face with Peter. The others drew back and formed a ring around them. For a long time, the two enemies just looked at each other.

"Proud youth," said Hook at last, "prepare to meet your doom."

"Come at me," replied Peter, not at all afraid.

Without further talk, they began to fight. Peter was a very good swordsman and was quick with his hands and feet. However, Hook could reach much farther with his sword. They fought for a long time, and it was unclear who would win this battle.

Then Peter lunged and pierced Hook's side. The pirate lost his footing and fell sideways, but then scrambled to get up. This was Hook's final moment. Peter moved slowly toward his opponent with his sword raised, and Hook jumped up on the side of the ship. With one kick, Peter pushed Hook into the sea. No one knew that the crocodile was waiting for him below.

And that was the end of Captain Hook.

Wendy had stood by, taking no part in the fighting. Now that it was over, she rejoiced that they had won. After a while, she found a clock in the cabin that read one-thirty in the morning! The fact that the boys were up hours and hours past their bedtime was the biggest event of all.

Wendy got the boys into the pirates' bunks pretty quickly that night—all except for Peter, who strutted up and down on the deck. He was too excited to sleep.

19

The Return Home

The next morning, they all put on pirate clothes with pants cut off at the knee. Of course, Peter was captain. Peter addressed the crew and asked that they do their jobs like "gallant hearties." They all cheered Peter loudly.

Back at home in London, where the Darling children had left so long ago, the window was still open. And now on the ship, John, Michael, and Wendy were planning their return home. They were looking forward to Mother's surprise, Father's shouts of joy, and Nana's leap through the air to embrace them.

Of course, their mother didn't need anyone to tell her to get things ready for the children. Everything was already waiting for them. The beds were aired, the window was left open, and Mrs. Darling was always at home, hoping her children would come back.

The only change in the nursery was that the kennel was now occupied by Mr. Darling. The reason why was that Mr. Darling felt it was his fault that the children had flown away—since none of it would have happened if he had not chained Nana up outside. He had had to admit that the dog was smarter than he.

So after the children had left, Mr. Darling went down on all fours and crawled into the kennel. Even when Mrs. Darling begged him to come out, he simply replied, "No, this is the place for me."

And so it was that Mr. Darling took the kennel to work with him every morning. He returned home taking the kennel with him every evening. Considering how he worried about what the neighbors thought, this was a very brave thing for Mr. Darling to do.

Soon people around town had heard what Mr. Darling was doing and why. He touched the hearts of many. Crowds followed him and his kennel everywhere. They cheered Mr. Darling in the streets. Important people invited him to dinner and wrote on the invitation, "Do come in the kennel."

On the night that the children came home, Mrs. Darling was in the night nursery, waiting for her husband. She was a sad-eyed woman now. She had not been happy since she lost her children.

Mrs. Darling had fallen asleep in her chair that night, but she awoke suddenly from a dream. "Oh, Nana," she said, "I dreamed the children came back." Nana put her paw gently in Mrs. Darling's lap to comfort her.

Mr. Darling soon came home from work and kissed his wife. His face was worn and saddened, too. Feeling drowsy himself, he curled up in the kennel and asked Mrs. Darling to play the piano for him.

Mrs. Darling went into the day nursery to play. And while she played, Mr. Darling slept. Suddenly Peter and Tinker Bell flew into the night nursery.

"Quick, Tink," Peter whispered, "close the window. So when Wendy comes, she will think her mother has locked her out and she will go back with me."

This plan had been in Peter's head all along. Peter was dancing with glee until he noticed that Mrs. Darling's playing had stopped. He peeked in on her and found she had laid her head on the piano. Tears fell slowly down her cheek.

She wants me to unlock the window, thought Peter, *but I won't.* He peeked at her again and saw that Mrs. Darling was still crying.

"She's awfully fond of Wendy," he said to himself. "But I'm fond of her, too. We can't both have her."

But Mrs. Darling's tears continued to fall, and Peter was unhappy. "Oh, all right," he said at last. He went and unlocked the window. "Come on, Tink," he said. "We don't want any silly mothers anyway." And they flew away into the night.

So Wendy and Michael and John found the window open for them after all. They landed quietly on the nursery floor.

"There's the kennel!" John cried, and dashed across the room to peek inside, thinking Nana would be in it.

But instead he said, "A man is inside."

"It's Father!" exclaimed Wendy.

"Surely he didn't used to sleep in a kennel . . ." wondered John.

"Perhaps we don't remember the old life as well as we thought," said Wendy. A chill fell upon them.

It was then that Mrs. Darling began playing again.

"It's Mother!" cried Wendy. She had a plan to tell their parents they were home. "Let us slip into our beds and be there when Mother comes in, just as if we had never been away."

And so when Mrs. Darling went to the night nursery to see if her husband was asleep, all the beds were filled. The children waited for her cry of joy, but it did not come. Although Mrs. Darling saw them, she did not believe they were there. She had dreamed about her children being home so often that she thought she was dreaming again.

Mrs. Darling sat down in her chair by the fire. The children could not understand this, and a cold fear welled up inside them.

"Mother!" cried Wendy.

"That's Wendy," Mrs. Darling said calmly. She was sure she was still dreaming.

"Mother!" called John.

"That's John," Mrs. Darling commented.

"Mother!" cried Michael.

"That's Michael," said Mrs. Darling, and she stretched out her arms for her three children she thought she would never hug again.

But instead of grasping the air she expected, her arms went around Wendy, John, and Michael, who had slipped out of bed and run to her. Then she knew she was not dreaming.

"George! George!" Mrs. Darling cried when she could speak. Mr. Darling awoke, and Nana came rushing in.

There could not have been a lovelier sight. But there was no one to see it except a little boy who was staring in through the window.

20

Peter Forgets

Now all of the lost boys had been waiting on the street below to give Wendy time to explain to her parents about them. But when they had counted to five hundred, the boys decided not to wait any longer. They went up the stairs instead of flying in the window because they thought this would make a better impression. As they stood in a row in front of Mrs. Darling, the boys wished they were not wearing their pirate clothes.

Of course, Mrs. Darling said at once that she would have them all. Mr. Darling went downstairs to set up space for them. As for Peter, Mrs. Darling told him that she would like to adopt him also.

"Would you send me to school?" asked Peter.

"Yes," she answered.

"And then to an office?" Peter wanted to know.

"I suppose so," Mrs. Darling said truthfully.

"Soon I would be a man?" Peter asked.

"Yes, very soon," replied Mrs. Darling.

"I don't want to be a man at all," Peter told her.

Mrs. Darling held out her arms for him, but Peter shrank back.

"Stay away," he said. "No one is going to catch me and make me a man."

"But where are you going to live?" asked Wendy.

"With Tink in the house we built for you. The fairies will put it in the treetops, where they sleep at night," Peter said, hoping Wendy would want to go with him.

"How lovely," replied Wendy. "May I go, Mommy?"

"Certainly not," was the answer. "I've got you home again, and I mean to keep you."

"But he does need a mother," said Wendy.

"So do you, love," Mrs. Darling reminded her. But she made an offer to both of them: Wendy could go visit Peter for a week every year to help him with his spring cleaning. Peter was delighted. The promise of Wendy's return sent him on his way quite satisfied.

"You won't forget me, will you, Peter?" Wendy asked to be sure.

"Of course not," he promised.

Once the boys were settled in, they all went off to school. They soon became as ordinary as any other children. It is sad to say that the power to fly slowly left them. They didn't practice. But the real reason they could not fly is that they no longer believed.

When Peter came for Wendy at the end of the first year, she wore the dress she had first flown away in. She hoped Peter would not notice that the dress had become too short for her.

Wendy had looked forward to talking about old times together, but new adventures had crowded out the old ones in Peter's mind.

"Who is Captain Hook?" he asked with interest when Wendy spoke of their last battle. Wendy was very surprised. And when she said she hoped that Tinker Bell would be glad to see her, Peter did not remember who Tink was either. Even when Wendy explained, Peter did not remember.

Even though the past year of waiting for Peter was a long one for Wendy, Peter felt as though it was yesterday. And then the next year, Peter did not come for her at all.

"Perhaps he is ill," Michael said. But Peter was never ill. He came the next spring and did not know that he had missed a year. That was the last time Wendy saw him again as a girl.

21

When Wendy Grew Up

The years came and went, and Wendy grew up and married. Of course, the boys all grew up as well. You could find the twins, Nibs, and Curly going to the office. Michael was an engine driver. Tootles became a judge. Slightly married, and so did John.

After a while, Wendy had a daughter, who was named Jane. They lived in the house she grew up in, and now Jane was in the nursery. Mrs. Darling and Nana had passed away, and Mr. Darling lived in a much smaller house now.

Wendy loved to tell her daughter stories at bedtime, and Jane had heard about Wendy's adventures in Neverland many, many times.

"Tell me how you flew when you were a little girl," Jane asked one night.

"Oh," Wendy answered, "I sometimes wonder if I ever did fly."

"Yes, you did," Jane insisted. "Why can't you fly now, Mother?"

"Because I am grown-up, dear," she said. "When people grow up, they forget the way."

"What was the last thing Peter said to you?" Jane asked.

"He said, 'Always be waiting for me, and then some night you will hear me crowing.' But alas, he has forgotten all about me," Wendy said with a smile, for it did not matter much to her anymore.

"What did the crow sound like?" asked Jane.

"It was like this," Wendy said, trying to imitate Peter.

"No, it wasn't," replied Jane. "It was like this." And she crowed much better than her mother. It sounded exactly like Peter.

Wendy was a little startled. "Darling, how did you know?"

"I often hear it when I am sleeping," Jane said calmly.

And then one night it happened.

Jane was asleep in her bed, and Wendy was sitting by the fire in the nursery. While Wendy sat, she heard Peter's crow. The window blew open, and Peter dropped on to the floor. He was exactly the same as ever. He was a little boy, but she was grown-up.

"Hello, Wendy," he said, not noticing that she was any different.

"Hello, Peter," she said faintly.

"Well, where is John?" Peter asked, looking around. "And Michael?" He glanced over at the bed where Jane slept.

"That is not Michael," said Wendy slowly.

"Is it a new one?" Peter asked.

"Yes, it is a girl," said Wendy, unsure if Peter would understand. "Peter, are you expecting me to fly away with you?" she asked.

"Of course," he answered. "That is why I have come." Then he added sternly, "Have you forgotten that it is spring-cleaning time?"

Wendy knew it was useless to explain to him that he hadn't come in years and years.

"I can't come," she said. "I have forgotten how to fly."

"I'll teach you again," replied Peter.

"Don't waste the fairy dust on me," Wendy pleaded. "I will turn up the light so you will see why." When she did so, Wendy could see that Peter was afraid. He gave a cry of pain when he saw the tall, beautiful woman in front of him.

"I am old, Peter," said Wendy. "I am much older than twenty. I grew up long ago."

"But you promised not to!" cried Peter.

"I couldn't help it," she explained. "I am married now, and the little girl in the bed is my child."

Peter took a step closer to the sleeping child. Then he sat down on the floor and began to cry. For the first time, Wendy did not know how to comfort him. She left the room to get him a handkerchief.

As Peter continued to cry, his sobs woke Jane, and

she sat up in bed.

"Boy," she said, "why are you crying?"

Just as he had done with her mother, Peter rose and bowed to Jane. She bowed in return from the bed.

"My name is Peter Pan," he said.

"Yes, I know," replied Jane.

"I came back for my mother," he explained, "to take her to Neverland."

"Yes, I know," Jane said. "I've been waiting for you."

When Wendy returned, she found Peter sitting on the bed crowing while Jane flew around the room with a smile on her face.

"She is my mother," Peter explained to Wendy as he pointed to Jane.

Jane returned gently to the floor. "He does so need a mother," she said.

"Yes, I know," admitted Wendy. "No one knows as well as I."

"Good-bye," Peter said to Wendy. And he rose in the air, and Jane rose with him.

Wendy rushed to the window. "No, no!" she cried.

"It is just for spring-cleaning time," Jane said.

"If only I could go with you." Wendy sighed.

Of course, in the end, Wendy let them fly away together. She watched out the window as the two flew up into the sky until they were as small as stars.

Jane is now a grown-up, and Wendy's hair has become white with age. Jane has a daughter named Margaret, and every spring-cleaning time, Peter comes for Margaret and takes her to Neverland.

When Margaret grows up, she will have a daughter who will be Peter's mother, too.

And so it will go on as long as children are children.